The Cat Who Knew the Meaning of Christmas

Written by
Marion Chapman Gremmels

Illustrated by
Dave LaFleur

Augsburg
MINNEAPOLIS

THE CAT WHO KNEW THE MEANING OF CHRISTMAS

Copyright © 1996 Augsburg Fortress. All rights reserved. Except for brief quotations in critical articles or reviews, no part of this book may be reproduced in any manner without prior written permission from the publisher. Write to: Permissions, Augsburg Fortress, 426 S. Fifth St., Box 1209, Minneapolis, MN 55440.

Cover and interior design by Elizabeth Boyce

ISBN 0-8066-2791-3

The paper used in this publication meets the minimum requirements of American National Standard for Information Sciences—Permanence of Paper for Printed Library Materials, ANSI Z329.48-1984.   ∞

Manufactured in the U.S.A.   AF 9-2791

00   99   98   97   96   1   2   3   4   5   6   7   8   9   10

For all who love cats and Christmas—
and for all who remember the author
as a loving, wise, and inspiring teacher.

Late one Christmas Eve,
Andrew was awake
and quiet in his bed.

The only sound he could hear was Cricket's purr
as she lay, warm and gentle on his chest.

Andrew wanted to close his eyes and sleep.
To stay awake, he needed to move, to stretch.
But he knew that if he twitched or wiggled,
Cricket would rise majestically, jump down,
and walk to her own bed in another room.

And Cricket must stay with him.
Only if Cricket stayed with him would he know. . .

Is the old story true?
Can all animals talk
during the secret stillness of midnight
on Christmas Eve?

Andrew's heavy eyelids closed.
He struggled to raise them.
It was almost midnight.

"Cricket," he whispered, "I can't go to sleep now.
Help me stay awake."
Cricket purred louder.
"Cricket, how can you be so calm?
If you really can talk at midnight, aren't you excited?"
Cricket's purr sounded like a song.
Andrew stroked her warm, soft back.
The purr seemed to separate into words.

"I am calm because it's Christmas, Andrew.
Christmas means everything to a cat.
Christmas means splendor, glory, wonder,
contentment, joy, and happiness.
Shall I sing you the story,
the story I sing my kittens,
the story my mother sang to me?"

"Oh, yes. Sing to me, Cricket," Andrew whispered.

"It all began in Bethlehem, long ago, in a stable that belonged to the Cat."

"Oh, Cricket, stables don't belong to cats," Andrew said.
Cricket glared at him.
She gathered her feet into a crouch,
ready to spring to the floor.
"I'm sorry, Cricket, please don't leave," Andrew cried.
"Please sing me your story."

Andrew scratched her neck, around and around,
hoping she would forgive him before midnight passed.
Cricket raised her head, inviting him
to scratch the itchy place under her chin.

Slowly, she let herself down on his chest.

"This stable belonged to the Cat.
She was an elegant black cat—very much like me.
The Cat worked hard to keep her stable tidy,
free of mice and rats.
Other animals came at night to eat and sleep,
sometimes oxen, sometimes donkeys,
sometimes sheep or goats.
But the Cat stayed always.

Every spring and fall,
the Cat's kittens were born
and she hid them
deep in an old manger,
in a warm, secret place under the grain box.
She fed them
and sang to them
and taught them the lessons
every kitten must learn.

When they were ready,
she let the kittens climb out of the manger
and find their own homes away from her stable.

One winter night,
the Cat heard busy noises in the town.

The innkeeper came into the stable.
She heard him say, 'Well, Joseph, it's only a stable,
but the Cat keeps it free of mice and rats,
and the hay is clean.
Sleep here if you like.'

The man with him said, 'It will do.
My wife is tired, and I must find some place for her to rest.'

The Cat watched Joseph lead a donkey into her stable.
He helped Mary down from the donkey's back.
Joseph made a bed in the hay for Mary.
He fed the donkey.

The night was quiet.
During the night,
a baby was born in the Cat's stable.

The Cat came from the corner to look.
The baby opened his eyes.
He looked at the Cat and smiled.

The Cat was happy and felt the warm feeling of love.

The Cat leaped into the old manger.
She showed Joseph the warm, secret place
under the grain box where she hid her kittens.
Joseph chuckled.
'Thank you, Cat,' he said.

Joseph tossed clean hay into the old manger.
Mary wrapped the baby in soft cloth.
Tenderly, Joseph laid him on the hay in the manger.
Mary slept, and Joseph slept near her.
The Cat lay beside the manger.
It was quiet.

Then the baby began to cry.
The Cat leaped into the grain box
at the top of the manger.
She looked over the edge at the baby.
She purred . . .
and the baby slept.
Then the Cat heard some wondrous music.

She heard singing in the starry night,
'Glory to God in highest heaven
and on earth peace and good will toward men!'

And so it was, Andrew,
that Jesus was born in the Cat's stable in Bethlehem.
That is why cats are calm,
cats are happy—
because they were blessed with the glory of Christmas love.
Christmas means everything to a cat."

"Oh, Cricket, thank you," Andrew whispered.
"Christmas means everything to a boy, too."
Cricket rose and jumped to the floor.
She turned toward Bethlehem,
and Andrew thought he could hear Cricket sing:
"Glory to God in highest heaven!"

Andrew climbed out of bed.
He faced Bethlehem.
He knelt beside Cricket.
"Glory to God in highest heaven!"
Andrew and Cricket sang together.

Cricket walked out of the room.

Andrew heard her running down the steps.
He hurried back to bed
and slid his feet under the warm covers.
He let his heavy eyelids close.